Published by Lumber and Building Material Dealers Foundation
Rensselaer, NY
www.nrla.org

For ordering information or special discounts for bulk purchases, please contact
Lumber and Building Material Dealers Foundation, 585 North
Greenbush Road, Rensselaer, NY 12144 or call 800-292-6752

Design and composition by Greenleaf Book Group LLC
Cover design by Greenleaf Book Group LLC
Illustrations by Randy Chewning

Publisher's Cataloging-In-Publication Data (Prepared by The Donohue Group, Inc.)
From tree to tree house : Chip and Emily's magic flume ride.—1st ed.
p. : col. ill. ; cm.
Summary: Emily and Chip take a ride on a magic flume to learn where lumber comes
from and about many of its uses. They discover the importance of using trees responsibly.
After they build a tree house with their father, they all plant another tree together.
Includes bibliographical references.
ISBN: 978-0-9829800-0-2
1. Lumber—Juvenile literature. 2. Wood products—Juvenile literature. 3. Forest
conservation—Juvenile literature. 4. Wood. 5. Lumber and lumbering. 6. Forest conservation.
I. Lumber and Building Material Dealers Foundation. II. Title: Tree to tree house
TS821 .F76 2011
67   2010935794

Part of the Tree Neutral™ program, which offsets the number of trees consumed in
the production and printing of this book by taking proactive steps, such as planting
trees in direct proportion to the number of trees used: www.treeneutral.com.

TreeNeutral®

Manufactured by Lehigh Phoenix on acid-free paper
Manufactured in Rockaway, New Jersey, USA, December 2010
Batch No. 1

10 11 12 13 14   10 9 8 7 6 5 4 3 2 1
First Edition

From TREE to TREE HOUSE

Chip and Emily's
MAGIC FLUME RIDE

To Donna, Bobby, and Scott

Today was the big day. Chip and Emily and their dad were going to build a tree house.

"Well," Dad said, "The first thing we need is lumber."

"Why do we need lumber?" Emily asked.

"We need lumber because lumber is the best material for building tree houses and people houses and dog houses and lots of other things, too."

"Where do we get lumber?"

"From our local lumber yard, Independent Lumber," Dad said. "Hop in the truck. Let's go."

"Hello everyone," said a smiling lady at Independent Lumber. "My name is Fern. How can I help you?"

"Hello, Fern," Dad said. "We need some lumber to build a tree house."

"We've got all kinds of lumber here," Fern said. "Long pieces and short piece. Wide pieces and narrow pieces."

"Where does all this lumber come from?" Emily asked.

"I was hoping you'd ask," Fern said. "Follow me."

"This is the magic flume," Fern said. "If you hop aboard, you'll meet all of my friends who will show you how we turn trees into lumber and many other things."

Emily was nervous. "Aren't you coming, Dad?"

"The magic flume is wonderfully safe," Dad said. "You are going to have a great adventure."

Chip and Emily fastened their seatbelts, and the magic flume took off.

The magic flume landed in a shady forest. Chip sniffed the cool air.

"Hi everyone," said a tall man in a hard hat. "I'm Fred the Forester. It's my job to take care of all the trees in this forest and choose just the right trees to turn into lumber."

"How do you choose?" Emily asked.

"We choose trees that are at just the right stage of growth, not too old and not too young. This one here, for example, is ready to be made into lumber."

Suddenly, they heard somebody shout from above: "Stand aside down there! Man in the tree."

Everyone moved a safe distance away from the tree and looked up.

"I'm Larry the Logger. I cut down the trees."

"Does that hurt the forest?" Emily asked. "I thought that cutting down trees was bad for the environment?"

"Not if I'm careful. I want to preserve the forest so that trees can grow here forever. I also want to be careful when I cut down trees on the tree farm."

"What's a tree farm?" Chip asked.

"Come with me."

"This is a tree farm," said Larry the Logger.

"Why are the trees all in a straight line?" Chip asked.

"Because that's the way we plant them, in straight rows. When the trees grow up, we harvest them, just like other farmers harvest their crops. Then we plant more trees. It's our responsibility to make sure that there are always plenty of trees for everyone."

"What happens to the trees after they are cut down?"

"The harvested trees are called logs. A big forklift picks up the logs and loads them onto a truck."

"Hang on, everyone!" shouted Tom the Trucker. "I'm headed down to the lumber mill in my new truck that runs on biodiesel."

The magic flume followed Tom the Trucker down the windy mountain road. Chip and Emily laughed when they saw a little bird hanging on tight to the magic flume.

A friendly lady at the lumber mill waved her hand. "Good driving, Tom," she said. "Welcome, everyone. I'm Mary the Mill Manager. I'm glad to see you are wearing hardhats."

"Mine feels a little funny," Emily said. "Why do we have to wear them?"

"Everyone wears hardhats for safety," Mary said. "The work here is very dangerous, and we want to make sure that no one gets hurt. You see, we take the logs from Tom's truck and put them on a conveyor belt. The logs move into the mill, where we cut them and shape them. Then they come out as lumber on the other side of the mill. I'll take you inside the mill, but first you must put in these earplugs."

"I don't hear much noise," Chip complained.

Mary smiled. "You will."

"We cut the lumber with powerful saws," Mary yelled. She had to talk loudly because the saws made so much noise. "Our workers have to be extremely careful, so that they cut the lumber to just the right size."

"Does this lumber go to our lumber yard?" Chip asked.

"You've got it," Mary said, nodding her head. "Some of the lumber goes to Independent Lumber, and some of it goes to different places all over the world."

Emily scratched her head. "Who decides where to send the lumber?"

"Just wait and see."

"Hey there, I'm Holly the Wholesaler. I sell the lumber from the mill to customers all around the world."

"And I'm Wally the Wholesaler. Holly and I work together."

Chip was confused. "But I don't see any lumber here."

"We don't move the lumber ourselves. We make sure that the right kind of lumber gets sold and delivered to the right person at the right time. You'll have to excuse me," said Wally. "I'm in the middle of filling an order from my friend Martin the Manufacturer. Can you make sure he gets the lumber he needs?"

Chip and Emily were excited. "We sure will."

"Thanks for your help," said Martin the Manufacturer. "This lumber will be perfect for making windows and doors."

"I thought you only used lumber to build houses." Chip said.

"Oh no," Martin said. "We use lumber to make all kinds of things."

"Furniture."

"Cabinets."

"Utility poles."

"Violins."

"Baseball bats."

"We are always coming up with new uses for wood, with the help of many, many people, like Ralph the Researcher."

"I'm Ralph the Researcher. I work with the Independent Lumber Association, an organization that has been around since 1894. We find new ways to turn trees into things we can use. I take cellulose from trees and make it into many different products. Like your school notebooks, film for the movies, even fabrics."

Emily was excited. "Can I wear a dress made of tree fabric?"

"Maybe someday," Ralph smiled. "Right now, it's time for you to return to the lumberyard. Bon voyage!"

Chip and Emily stood outside the lumberyard.

"Where did the magic flume go?" Chip asked.

"It went back inside the lumberyard, ready for another adventure. I'm Carlos the Carpenter. I'm using lumber to build Fern's new house."

"This doesn't look like a house," Chip said.

"This is what we call the frame of a house. It keeps the house standing up straight and strong. My friend over there is putting up the walls. Later we will put on the roof, then it will look like a house."

"I hope our tree house looks like a house," Chip sighed.

"I'm sure it will," Carlos the Carpenter said. "Your dad is quite a good carpenter. In fact, he's inside the lumberyard right now, waiting for you. I think he's ready to take you home and start building."

When they saw their Dad, Chip and Emily took turns telling him all about their adventure.

"Dad, we flew in the magic flume and learned how we get lumber from trees," said Emily.

"Fred the Forester selects the trees in the forest," said Chip.

"Larry the Logger harvests the trees and plants new ones."

"Tom the Trucker drives the logs to the Mill."

"Mary the Mill Manager cuts the logs into lumber."

"Holly and Wally the Wholesalers send the lumber all over the world.

"Ralph the Researcher discovers new things to make out of trees."

"And Carlos the Carpenter builds houses."

"Maybe someday you two will be able to work with the people you met in the lumber industry," Dad said.

"That would be great," Emily said, clapping her hands.

Chip asked with excitement, "Can we start today?"

"I'm afraid you'll have to wait a few years," Dad said. "But right now, let's go home. We've got a tree house to build."

Chip and Emily watched carefully as Dad cut the lumber to just the right size and hammered it together. Then they all painted the tree house a bright green.

"We're all done," Chip said.

"Not quite yet," Dad said. "We have one more thing to do."

Dad brought out a young tree. Chip and Emily helped Dad plant the young tree in the backyard.

"We always have to remember that trees are a valuable resource," Dad said. "When this tree grows up, it will give us lots of shade."

"And we'll be able to build another tree house in it," Chip said.

"And then we'll plant another tree," Emily added.

"I'm proud of you," Dad said. "You've learned how we continue the cycle. We use trees wisely now and plant more trees for the future. Now who wants to have a cool drink of lemonade?"

GLOSSARY

BIODIESEL: A fuel for cars and trucks that is made exclusively from vegetable oil or animal fats.

CELLULOSE: All kinds of plants, trees, and flowers make cellulose. Cellulose makes stems and branches strong enough to support even the tallest trees.

HARVEST: Foresters harvest, or remove, trees when the trees are ready to bring to market, just as farmers harvest their crops.

MILL: A building with special machines that saw logs into standard-size boards and timbers.

PRESERVE: A special piece of land that is reserved and managed for the protection and study of plants and animals.

RESEARCHER: A person who investigates the use of the forest's resources to determine the best way to grow trees and use forest products.

TREE FARM: An area of forest in which the growth of the trees is managed to make sure that trees are always growing there and that animal homes and water supplies are protected.

WHOLESALE: The term used to describe the sale of goods by manufacturers and others to retailers who then resell the goods to the general public.